VAMPIRE

For (in order of chronological involvement) Malcolm Griffiths, Anna Mottram, Di Patrick, Dusty Hughes, Lori Larsen, Richard Romagnoli and Susan Sharkey.

Snoo Wilson

VAMPIRE

AMBER LANE PRESS

All rights whatsoever in this play are strictly reserved and
application for permission to perform it in whole or in part
must be made in advance before rehearsal to:

Goodwin Associates
19 London Street
London W2.

No performance may be given unless a licence has been
obtained.

First published in 1979 by
Amber Lane Productions Ltd.,
Amber Lane Farmhouse,
The Slack,
Ashover, Derbyshire S45 0EB.

Printed in Great Britain by
A. Wheaton & Co. Ltd., Exeter.

Typesetting and make-up by
Computerset (Phototypesetting) Ltd., Oxford.

Copyright © Snoo Wilson, 1979

ISBN 0 906399 11 4

Front cover photograph: Chris Davies (Report)

Vampire was written specially for Paradise Foundry, who gave the first production of the play at the Oval House, London, on 28 April, 1973. It was directed by Malcolm Griffiths and performed by the following members of the company:

Nicholas Ball
Michael Harrigan
Anna Mottram
Diana Patrick
Mark Penfold
Pat Rossiter

Vampire

When I first started writing plays with the subsequent trickle into publication, I felt rather snooty about authorial prologues as I believed the structures of the plays should make themselves known to the reader without sackfuls of didactic autobiography being poured upon him. My plays, I thought, were for performance, demonstrations of an aesthetic in action, and anyhow I wasn't too sure of what I or they said, when we were put on the spot and made to stand still and declare our intentions. However, this current publication of *Vampire* was offered with the proviso of an introduction so I feel quite free to sing for my supper, freedom being the recognition of necessity in this case.

Malcolm Griffiths was running a company of three men and three women, who invited me to write a play. I wanted to write a play that spanned a century and although I had only a very hazy idea of where it all would end, I knew where it would start, which was in a Welsh Non-conformist parsonage, where a weak, pragmatic father was trying to bring up three girls on his own, with the past interfering in the shape of his wife's suicide and the future tugging at the family in the shape of the fabulous energy of the towns which were springing up like mushrooms all over England. And of course I wanted to write about London, the Great Wen, whose growth so spectacularly converted people into two sorts: those who lived in it and those who didn't: a city of refugees, from the country. And this seems to be a version of the story which the human race has talked itself to sleep with all along. Christians and Jews think they've been pushed out of the Garden of Eden. The Eskimos have a belief that they were not originally from the northern latitudes but were constrained to live there. (I remember this anthropological delicacy because it was explained in a book on flying saucers I read that the Eskimos had been banished from Atlantis and were dropped in the less hospitable regions by flying saucers. Stalin, it seems, was not the first to use the frozen north for getting rid of those who were too awkwardly shaped to fit through the grid marked 'citizen'.)

In the three acts of the play, separated by fifty years, I have tried to show the masks of style and oppression and their relativity to an age. In the second act the women in the play are linked by a weak memory — a half-admitted scandal of incest in the family — to the Joy of the first act. The women have become apparently paradigms of Edwardian frankness about the possibility of marrying for money and yet the First World War, which used to be called 'Great' till we had another one, sweeps them in different directions. Anthea's husband, who is killed in the war, returns as a ghost to the imprisoned Sarah, who with great clarity of vision and purpose has been setting fire to churches, in the middle of the First World War, to try and get women the vote. And the only thing I had to invent about this part of the story was the ghost. There were women who weren't sucked into the war fever machine, and went the other way. I had them meet ghosts.

Jung and Freud are summoned after the ghostly impregnation to provide doctorly help to the pregnant Sarah, who has become the Mary in a contemporary nativity play. I don't think this is an injustice to these great figures, though it may be a sidelong tribute to place them in their own time. Freud lost a son in the First World War. As an old man his international connections managed to save his life from the Nazi concentration camps, and he was spared that horror to die in London of the cancer from which he had been suffering for two decades. Before he left he was made to sign a paper saying that the Nazis had not maltreated or abused him. He signed it, and added at the bottom with terrifying humour: "I can recommend the SS to anyone".

Jung, who became the renegade and rival of Freud after having been the good *goy* of the Vienna circle, was the focus of a truly wonderful event which was recorded on camera on a programme on his life. Some time after his death a commentator was standing summing up the last of a series of programmes on the great man. He was standing, he told the camera, by the house that Jung had archetypally built for himself, beside *the* mountain, with the archetypal lake visible behind. Suddenly the admiring but necessarily light television summary was interrupted by growls of thunder. The speaker, Laurens van der Post, immediately incorporated this into his commentary, saying what a *Jungian* thing to happen that was, and they kept the cameras rolling while the dead man (if indeed it was him) boomed and thundered, stronger than words, across the calm surface of the Swiss lake.

The third act of the play is to do with people who live in the present, or attempt to, and thus find themselves catering for all the old bogies all over again. Freud's assertion that originally all the dead were vampires who had a grudge against the living and sought to rob them of their lives, comes out as another anthropological delicacy, born of a perusal of *The Golden Bough* rather than any direct experience of field work in primitive anthropology. And yet it's true enough of the here and now: we are always telling each other that those who do not understand history are condemned to repeat it, or we trot out the Marxist chestnut about history happening the first time as tragedy and the next time as farce. While agreeing about the repetition of history, I'd take exception to the idea that history is ever any one thing. Tragedy implies the high style, without the double edge of comedy. Tragedy implies high-minded purposes in conflict, a style of taking oneself extremely seriously as the suffering hub of the universe. In the third act tragic suffering (death on the roads) is cynically democratised into do-it-yourself religion for junkies. People's self-absorption has become so great that they accept the most obvious outside manipulations and sham shamanisms: it is a singular event when women are able to become priests, as in the third act, but unless they free themselves from the *style* of handing religion down to the grateful flock they are going to be still tied to the past. Style is power but power corrupts, and politics, as Emerson observed, is a deleterious profession. But there is also nothing which is free of style, of history. Artists who are drawn to the 'primitive' because of its apparent lack of associations with sophisticated contradictions are simply adding another trophy to the jumble of objects in the much fought over warehouse where civilisation is rumoured to reside.

The third act has troubled me for some time and I have rewritten it till I was quite sick of it. When a group in South Africa wanted to do the play I agreed on condition that they perform my South African third act. I wrote it and they never did the completed piece but Dusty Hughes rescued it from its orphaned condition and it became a separate play called *Soul of the White Ant*. I wrote a further third act for a recent London production, which was a fair attempt to use new cloth to patch an old cape.

In the most recent production in New York they decided they preferred the old third act and so I salved my conscience by adding a long wordless scene to the beginning, which I have included in this edition. The last speech, however, is like the bleeding stump of an amputee that refuses to heal. Until its rhetoric goes out of fashion it should be played by whoever, in the public eye, speaks the vampiric language of the dead and the undead, of the them-and-us — whether the local bogey is the Ayatollah Khomeini, or Colonel Sanders ubiquitously springing Kentucky Fried Chicken on the innocents of the street. I hope it is a fitting end to the play to take these modern totems, these media ghosts, and to test their credibility by giving them an actor's flesh and a politician's words.

Artists are supposed to be revered because they apparently create something out of nothing (a triumph of capitalism) or, like paranoiacs, they most burdensomely imagine things that aren't there, depending on your point of view of whether you think art is good for you. *I* desperately want my art to be good for people. I'd like it to come stamped with gold medals for purity and excellence, like my favourite mango chutney. I'd like its nourishing qualities to be immediately obvious. I am afraid of putting in too many stage directions, or not enough. I am writing about and for people but people are full of ghosts; paranoia begins at home, and to extrapolate at all I am obliged to follow the iron law of the imagination. I hope, in this instance, the ghosts on offer are digestible.

Snoo Wilson
August, 1979

ACT ONE: Scene One

Characters

JOY
RUTH
JESSE
DAVIS *A Welsh parson, their father*
REUBEN *Ruth's fiance*
GARETH *A serving man*
VAMPIRE
CHARLES DICKENS

SCENE ONE

A table and chair stage left are lit in one pool.
Stage right another pool of light with a bed in
it. A bell tolls and the lights on stage slowly
die. Finally there is a blackout. The bell stops.

Three girls in long white Victorian night-
dresses come on from stage left. One of them
has a candle. They stop at the table. Plainly,
they are in a mischievous mood.

JOY: Look, it's Da's diary.

RUTH: Don't read it.

JESSE: No, we shouldn't read it.
        [*They all crowd round and look at it.*]
        Lord, it's boring, all cattle markets and
        sermons ...

JOY: Here — what's this tiny writing —? 'Lord
        forgive me, without the succour of a wife I ...'
        and then it gets really tiny '... formed the deed
        of darkness with Mrs Plum, an English-
        woman who was raising money by subscrip-
        tions for an iron-frame chapel for the
        Colonies, upon a *tombstone* ...'
        [RUTH *snatches the diary away.*]

RUTH: That's disrespectful.

JOY: What's a deed of darkness?
        [RUTH *puts the diary back on the*
        table.]

JESSE: What Evan does with the sheep.
        [*Laughing and chatting, they move*
        round the set and climb into bed.]

RUTH: Don't you tax him with it neither.

> [JOY *makes shapes on* RUTH'*s back as
> she combs her hair — shadows with
> her hands from the candle.*]

JESSE: It's a bat.

  JOY: No, it's a man.

> [JOY *and* JESSE *laugh.*]

JESSE: It's a sea monster.

  JOY: No, it's a land monster.

JESSE: [*making one*] Here, look, Evan with his dick
       up — Oh, I'm going to die of fright.

> [JOY *and* JESSE *laugh and* RUTH
> *hushes them angrily.*]

       I'm dead already — tell us a story, Joy ...

  JOY: After the French invasion of Wales, they hung
       a monkey because they thought he was a
       Frenchman, with his long, long tail ...

> [*They all laugh.*]

       There was a king who had three lovely
       daughters ...

RUTH: What! Again!

  JOY: [*unstoppable*] ... with dresses as white as
       snow, and each one was as shimmering and
       beautiful as the other in her own peculiar way
       ... They were so lovely that even the sea
       monsters, when the daughters took a stroll
       down to the whelk stall on the sands, felt
       deliciously squirmy down in their deep muddy
       holes, and at low tide the conger eels stood on
       their hindquarters and hoarsely barked their
       approbation ... But there was one trouble
       with these beautiful daughters, that they were
       locked up in a great tomb of ice, and no one
       could get at them ...

JESSE: How did they get the sea monsters squirmy
       then?

JOY: Oh, their Da let them out just once, one sunny day, but that was all. Anyhow, nobody could get at them because they lived in the far frozen North ...

RUTH: [*practical*] They could have moved south, to Carmarthen ...

JOY: No! They loved it in Iceland, because it was so sad and icy, and they were all languid and passive, and they lay with their sweet frozen little hands, all cold.

> [*They rub their hands in front of the candle.*]

Their tiny cherry mouths, their demure downcast eyes, and their soft skin which the servants marvelled at when they came to wash their marbled bodies, in still water, in marble baths, in marble halls, where only drippings disturbed the silence of eternity.

JESSE: Didn't they have jokes?

JOY: No! Their father, the king of Iceland, came in and frightened them half to death with horrid stories, about blood, and spiders and Jews, and Roman Catholics, and it was night all the time there, and the sheeted dead gibbered in the streets. [*Pause.*] Gibbered in the streets. And they were all locked in the ice. Three sisters, three princesses, waiting for a beautiful prince. And one night as they were waiting — a thing — with teeth and claws, and sharp ripping and biting and tearing and gouging and blood-red eyes and teeth, and this thing, came tap-tapping at the outside of the ice — and — they saw its face peering through, eager, beseeching, and promising not to hurt them, and they knew if they let it in, they would have to follow it for ever, and it had a big cloak to hide its wickedness in, and it tapped outside where the ice was thinnest, and a sudden fatal drowsy warmness suffused them, and they knew that if they moved it would go away, but they could not move, because they were so cold, and as they got warmer and warmer the ice began to melt away — and the thing — came in!

[RUTH *puts the candle out and they all scream.*]

RUTH: Let's go to sleep now.

[*Lights up on the bed. Standing by it is* DAVIS, *the parson, their father, dressing.*]

DAVIS: A lot of noise last night ...

[*Pause.*]

What worries me chiefly about your tender minds and bodies is that, having been without a mother for so long, you have found me rather more convincing as a father than as a mother. I seem to have brought you up as boys. [*Pause.*] Fighting at meals. [*Pause.*] Biting each other in bed. [*Pause.*] Whipping each other to a pitch of un-Christian excitement, when you are meant to be reposing. Too much wild education, and not enough discipline. Within a few years you girls will probably have your hands asked for in marriage. Now if you want a happy marriage it will not be by outsmarting your husband, or by biting him. Men find this hateful in a woman. Your function is child-bearing, and a demure acquiescence in other matters that do not concern you. You are poor.

If you ever go to London and move into society, there will be people there who will find your previous dormitory arrangements risible. If you want to marry above you, keep your mouth shut. Do not let your frivolous imagination run riot. You must forbear profane thoughts. You must grieve more — the world is not to be taken lightly; govern your thoughts into socially useful or decorative channels. Of the three of you, Ruth is the only one who has ever tried her hand at embroidery. Society has no place for active lunatics. They are no more use than mice, horsing about in the scullery when the rest of the house has gone about its business. So don't let's have any more cloaked men in the broom cupboard with sharp teeth. Tell them to go and try somewhere else, eh?

[*Blackout. Then* DAVIS *comes into the spot.*]

Oh God, preserve us from all wicked and scandalous thoughts for we know in our heart of hearts that to imagine them is to Thy mind, which sees our innermost workings, the same as actually having consummated them. For the sake of Thy only son Jesus, who was crucified virginal without resistance and offered his blood for our sake, Amen.

[*Spot out. The lights go up.* JESSE *and* JOY *are in the bed.* RUTH *and* DAVIS *have gone. The lights are much dimmer than before.*]

JESSE: Your feet are cold and wet.

JOY: I'll warm them on your bum, then.

[*She does so.* JESSE *turns and pinches her.*]

Ah!

JESSE: Shut up or we'll have another row with Da.

JOY: He's giving Ruth his bedroom and he's going to have to sleep in the barn!

[*They both laugh.*]

He'll come up and tell us to stop being savages.

JESSE: People always sleep on their own in big houses.

JOY: But she's marrying a corporal from Aberdovey. He won't have a big house ... Will you miss me when I go, Jess?

JESSE: Suppose I go before you?

JOY: Well, I'm sixteen, and I'm prettier than you are.

[JESSE *pinches her.*]

JESSE: Go back to sleep.

[*They lie back on their backs.*]

JOY: You know why my feet are cold. I went out to the bottom of the garden and swung out on the swing over the graves just when the sun was going down, and the air was cold and heavy in the yew tree and there were spiders — and the whole world was utterly still — and suddenly I got really warm all of a sudden and I swung and I swung and it got really nice, sweeter and warmer, and then it was ever so sweet and warm and I stopped, and the sun went down in glory ...

JESSE: [*with awful severity*] That wasn't the sun, that was your cat. You'll go to hell for that — or go blind like Jonesy.

JOY: Women don't go blind for that — men go blind

because it goes green and drops off. That's
common knowledge.

JESSE: If you go on like that I shall tell Da.

> [*The lights cross out to a set piece
> round the piano.* GARETH, *the serving
> man, is sitting at the piano.* RUTH *is
> about to sing.* DAVIS *looks on
> admiringly and takes snuff.* REUBEN, *a
> corporal, is ready to turn the pages of
> the song-book for* GARETH. *He is
> looking admiringly at* RUTH. RUTH
> *sings,* GARETH *plays.* REUBEN *sings
> harmony.*]

RUTH: 'I know —
That my —
Re-dee-mer
Liveth . . .'

JESSE: [*off*] If mother was alive I don't know what
she'd say.

JOY: [*off*] Well, she's not!

JESSE: She'd die of shame if she were.

JOY: The result would be the same — then!
[*They fall into the tableau.*]

JESSE: [*over the singing still*] Da! Joy's been playing
with her cat!
[*The singing stops.*]

DAVIS: [*sternly*] We haven't got a cat. Back to bed, the
pair of you.

JESSE: [*to* JOY] I know what's going to happen to
you! You're going to be a scarlet woman in
London.
[*The singing starts at the beginning
again.*]

RUTH: 'I kn-ow
That m-y
[*furiously*] Redeemer liveth.'

JOY: It felt natural enough to me!

JESSE: Not even the servants do it!

            [JOY *blows a raspberry at* JESSE.]

DAVIS: Stop that you two — get back to bed or I'll give you a hiding — you're a little slut Joy —

JOY: [*raising her nightdress at the tableau*] Bugger off, the lot of you!

            [REUBEN *and* RUTH *stop in mid-bar. Tableau.*]

RUTH: [*weakly*] I'm going to faint.

JESSE: Ah, come on, you've seen that trick before, love
. . .

            [RUTH *duly faints. The menfolk gather round and revive her.*]

DAVIS: Jesse, you stay here. Joy, you will go to your room and remain there till called. Gentle society cannot take that sort of madness.

            [JOY *goes.* JESSE *stays.* RUTH *gets up again. The song starts again, with all of them singing.*]

RUTH: 'I kn----ow
That my —
Redeem-er
Leeeeeveth —'

            [*Blackout.*]

            [*Lights up on the bed where* JOY *is reading poetry. The music continues, on the piano, but* RUTH *does not sing.*]

JOY: 'Sooner or later I too may take the print of the golden age —

Why not? I have neither hope nor trust.
May make my heart as a millstone, set my face
                                    as a flint —
Cheat and be cheated and die — who knows
We are ashes and dust.'

> [*The music finishes.* GARETH *goes off,
> the rest sit round the table.* DAVIS *goes
> and stands in the dark between the two
> spots.* JOY *goes and takes off her night-
> dress and does a few poses in front of
> an imaginary mirror. She holds her
> hair back.*]

'What should I be at fifty
Should nature keep me alive
If I find the world so bitter
When I am but twenty-five?'
Well ... sixteen ...

> [DAVIS *goes and sits gloomily on the
> bed, facing away from* JOY. JOY
> *pointedly ignores him. The lights
> come up on the table.* JESSE, RUTH *and*
> REUBEN *are seated round it.*]

JESSE: We got in touch with Mother once ... Da
won't do it, says it's wicked, playing with the
spiritual world. But if they're there I think they
ought to talk to us.

> [*They place their fingertips on the
> table.*]

REUBEN: Are the dead resentful?

JESSE: Oh no, they just find it difficult to be tactful,
and quite often their spelling's bad.

REUBEN: Are they in Heaven?

RUTH: Oh, they *must* be in Heaven. I *know* Mama is
in Heaven.

REUBEN: What do we do if your father comes aback and finds us here?

JESSE: We say we're playing cards. Hands on the table now. Is there anybody there? Anybody there?
> [*They freeze. The other tableau activates.*]

DAVIS: [*still facing away from* JOY, *who is facing away from him*] Cover your shame, you mad hussy.
> [*She sulkily gets into bed.*]

What you have done has outlawed you from society. You have brought a taint of satanic lunacy which I thought this family was rid of. We shall never be able to let you out again unaccompanied. You must count yourself fortunate to belong to the literate classes. Were we poor, or unenlightened, or superstitious, we would have had to send you to the new Bedlam.
> [*He exits, sadly, and goes into the other area. He sees the seance.*]

What are you playing at?

JESSE:
RUTH: } Whist, father.

DAVIS: [*gathering up the cards*] Watch and pray. Do not let the devil into this house.
> [*He exits from the stage.*]

JOY: [*lying in bed*] I'm bored. I'm bored.
> [*She gets out of bed. A terrific scream.*]

I'm bored!
> [*Everybody looks round instantly. JOY's room is in darkness.*]

JESSE: [*breathless*] Are you good or evil? Knock once for good, twice for evil.

                         [JOY *listens, delighted.*]
RUTH: I'm frightened — it might be lying . . .
JESSE: No, that'll be all right, we can go on now . . .
                         [*Two thumps.*]
          We can't?
RUTH: Ask it if we're in love . . .
                         [*One thump.*]
          Forever?
                         [*One thump.*]
          And our wedding day will be glorious . . .
                         [*One thump.*]
JESSE: Do you recite the Lord's Prayer backwards?
  JOY: [*thoughtfully*] Do I recite the Lord's Prayer
          backwards . . .? A-nema . . . reve dna yrolg . . .
          glogry . . . [*shouting*] No, I don't think I do!
                         [REUBEN *stands.*]
REUBEN: There is fraud here. Those noises are coming
          from upstairs.
                         [*One thump.*]
RUTH: Don't leave — I'm frightened — dearest.
                         [*She grabs at him. One thump.*
                         REUBEN *goes to the bedroom.* JOY
                         *surprises him from behind and they
                         fall on the bed.* RUTH *bursts into tears
                         and stifles it to listen. She and* JESSE
                         *hold each other. The thumpings start
                         again. This time it is* REUBEN *and* JOY
                         making love.]
  JOY: Aah —
RUTH: They're speaking in tongues!
                         [*The sounds of love-making continue.*
                         JESSE *becomes frightened and runs off
                         shouting to fetch* DAVIS.]
JESSE: Da! Da! Da! We got a devil, I'm very sorry —

             [*She exits.*]

RUTH: Oh — don't leave me!

             [RUTH, *the only lit figure on the stage, starts to become hysterical.*]

JOY: [*independent, curious in the dark to* REUBEN] You a vampire? When you going to bite me then?

RUTH: [*now entirely hysterical*] Aaaaah!

JOY: [*joyfully*] Oh, you naughty old vampire you!

             [*The knockings climax and stop.* JESSE *comes galloping back, pushing* DAVIS, *who holds the cross out in front of him.*]

JESSE: Oh quick!

DAVIS: Avaunt! Avaunt! Aschitophel!

JESSE: No, it's Dracula, Da!

DAVIS: They all answer to the same name! Avaunt, anyhow!

JESSE: I'll get some garlic!

DAVIS: No! We run out!

             [*He goes to* RUTH *and holds out the cross tremblingly.*]

Leave this woman, I command you!

RUTH: [*frothing and rolling on the table*] In the water — he held me — in baptism — his hard strong chill fingers — so young was I — he bent my bones, and drew the marrow from them — more than a handful — putty of the flesh for our Lord to fill — mould into a chamber for his graces — and he came — the cruel grasp of his fingers — and he drew blood — the stench of the charnel house — twenty men's force — and the strength of death — *judgement* ...

DAVIS: Come on, Jesse, get her into the church to sober up!

JESSE: But he'll take Reuben —

DAVIS: He's all right, he's a soldier —

[*They drag and push* RUTH *off into the wings, leaving the seance area empty. A distant shriek from* RUTH. *Slowly, hand in hand,* JOY *and* REUBEN *come into the lit square. They are dressed,* REUBEN *in his uniform again and* JOY *in her nightdress.* REUBEN *is emotionally shattered and sits down heavily at the table with his head on his arm, taking his hand away from* JOY. JOY *looks at him. She is feeling quite bright.*]

JOY: Come on, old moany.

[*She takes his hand and he removes it. She glances round, looking for something to distract his attention. She drums her fingers on the table, whistles a little tune.*]

Bum ti bum ti bum ti ... nice funeral parlour you have here ...

REUBEN: [*muffled*] Ruined ...

JOY: Well, there's always a first time.

[REUBEN *raises his head.*]

REUBEN: This is painful for both of us.

[JOY *sits on his knee.*]

JOY: Oh, I don't know ...

REUBEN: I don't know what came over me. I cannot begin to apologise and I shall carry your silent reproaches to the end of my days.

JOY: [*piqued*] They won't be silent in a bit, either.

[*She kisses him.*]

REUBEN: It's no use pretending that we behaved any better than animals — I cannot damn myself more than that — I can only assure you that when I stood at the bottom of the stairs I was full of the spirit of scientific enquiry. Perhaps that Darwin is right and we are descended from apes.

JOY: [*now annoyed*] Oh, go and climb a tree, then.
> [*She gets off his knee and goes to the table. She puts her hand on the table in a mock seance position.*]

Is there anybody there? Anybody there? [*Pause.*] Apparently not. [*Pause.*] Look, I always asked for Dracula when I was in bed, but I don't mind a substitute.

REUBEN: I should shoot myself.

JOY: I think he likes them timorous, a bit quieter than me.
> [*She sings in plummy mimicry of* RUTH.]

'I know —
That my —
Redeemer —
Liveth —'

REUBEN: Stop it!

JOY: Where are they all then? Have they been taken off by big red sheep into the mountains?
> [REUBEN *raises his head.*]

REUBEN: If I leave, or if I end my life, it is the only thing which will preserve sanity and civilisation — I hate to think how I have inflicted my will upon you.

JOY: You ask Da, he'll tell you I'm a noisome voluptuary.

[*Pause. She imitates* DAVIS.]
Just like little dogs.

REUBEN: How can I look your sister in the face ...?

JOY: [*mock ingenuous*] I don't know, with that squint she's got on her.

REUBEN: Perhaps if I went on a mission to savages ... except there is no difference between us. I suppose I have a gnawing remorse, which is better than a profound ignorance of all virtues. At least we have no idols.

[JOY *gets up, bored.*]

JOY: I'm going back to bed — if anything happens, I'll say it was Dracula, except I don't think he comes out this far.

[DAVIS *re-enters, still brandishing the cross and leading a sobbing* RUTH, JESSE *bringing up the rear.* RUTH *is wearing her wedding head-dress, at a rakish angle.*]

DAVIS: Hence! Hence!

[RUTH *collapses at* REUBEN'*s feet. She raises her arms to him.*]

RUTH: Am I — still beautiful ... beautiful ...?

[*She strokes her own face.*]

Will you take me — for ever ...?

[REUBEN *is hideously embarrassed.*]

For ever and ever and ever ... [*Pause.*] Staining the white radiance of eternity ...

[JOY *laughs, inappropriately.*]

DAVIS: Get to your room, Joy.

RUTH: [*still going at* REUBEN] A sign — a sign that you have loved me — my love — your hands are as cold as ice — your eyes are as cold as ice — and your mouth is as cold as ice ...

[JOY *shrugs.*]

I'm so frightened — marry me, Reuben — marry me now . . .

REUBEN: What? *Now?*

> [*There is an agonised pause.* DAVIS *looks round distractedly for something to ease the strain of living. He sees that* JOY *has still not gone.*]

DAVIS: You're to do with this. So help me Lord, I'm going to chastise you. I'm going to take the skin off your back until you see some sense.

> [JOY *backs behind the piano.*]

JOY: I'll run away!

DAVIS: You won't do that either. Jess, go and get a big strong ashplant from the woodshed.

> [*He grabs* JOY's *wrist.*]

You come along with me. [*calling*] Gareth! We're going to have a wedding!

> [*Exeunt* JOY *and* DAVIS, *and* JESSE. RUTH *and* REUBEN *stand up together.* GARETH, *a serving man, comes in and sits at the piano. Beside him stands* JESSE, *who brings a cloth and crucifix to put on the table.* RUTH *and* REUBEN *line up as if in front of an altar.* DAVIS *re-enters the lit part with an extremely sulky* JOY, *whom he leads by a handcuff. He handcuffs her to* GARETH, *who has to play the piano as well.*]

GARETH: But . . .

DAVIS: Look after her for me, Gareth.

> [*He goes and stands in front of the couple.*]

GARETH: [*looking dispassionately at his handicap*]

Never was much good with my left hand,
anyway ...
          [*He plays the tune of* I know that my
          Redeemer liveth.]

DAVIS: [*over the piano*] Who giveth this woman to be
married to this man? In the absence of Cor-
poral Beesdon of the True Church of the
Revived Faith, she will have to give herself.
          [*He leans forward.*]
You do give yourself? Reuben Mavros?
          [RUTH *nods.* DAVIS *looks at* REUBEN,
          who nods.]
You too? Right, pronounce your marriage
vows.
          [JOY *leads the piano player disgrace-*
          fully astray by lifting his left hand
          high above his head. He brings it
          down with a mighty effort, crashing
          into the keys.]
Mother of God. Stop that confounded racket
you two! [*barely audible*] To ... love honour
and obey him in all corporal as well as
spiritual matters ... [*The rest is lost.*]

REUBEN: To take holy orders and go and pronounce the
true faith amongst savages.

DAVIS: [*savagely*] You won't have to move hardly a
step, boy.
          [*A genteel pause.*]
Very good. I pronounce you man and wife.
          [*He makes a determined effort to pull*
          the event together. GARETH *starts to*
          play the Wedding March. JOY *pulls*
          him away from the piano and they
          exit.]

[*abruptly*] Amen!
> [*He exits,* RUTH *and* REUBEN *are left frontstage in front of the impromptu altar. He moves to kiss her and at that moment she darts away and the lights go off.*]

> [*A huge chant of Welsh hymn singing, an enormous congregation bursting its lungs, two choruses.* DAVIS *comes forward to a spot frontstage. The music dies away. He addresses the audience. He is also working hard to convince himself.*]

DAVIS: [*a homily*] It is good . . . [*Pause.*] . . . to work in the cities, the infernos of our time which consummate the frail souls of humanity, like paper, into the everlasting furnace. To read the Bible to the poor benighted illiterates who have fallen under that dreadful Juggernaut, the treadmill of factory ownership. God has called many of us to the service of the hearthside. To succour and comfort our fellow men. In this we are all blessed. How much worthier is it, then, to bear the flaming brand of Christ's teaching into souls so defiled by ignorance that they are like unto a dark faceless tablet of evil . . . Wash their souls white in the blood of the lamb that knows no sin! Purify them with his body! A nation, the richest nation on the face of the earth, in the history of the world, has a duty to send its sons to areas of savagery.
> [*Triumphant. The piano stops in mid-phrase.*]

In Africa, black Africa, there are many, many
more souls to be won!

> [*Blackout on his triumphant face.*
> *Cross cut to the bed, where* REUBEN
> *and his deathly pale bride are. They*
> *are facing away from each other. Very*
> *slowly, with great agony of spirit,*
> REUBEN *draws his boot off.* RUTH *lays*
> *aside her bridal veil equally slowly.*
> *She measures out a huge dose of*
> *chloral and drinks it. (Chloral is a*
> *colourless liquid.)* REUBEN *goes round*
> *to her side of the bed, un-booted. He*
> *picks up the bottle.*]

REUBEN: What's this?

RUTH: Chloral.

REUBEN: What?

RUTH: It helps me sleep more easily. I have the most
terrible dreams of . . . burglars . . . murderers —
coming in through the window . . .

> [*She gets up suddenly and they em-*
> *brace mechanically.*]

REUBEN: I'll save you from them. [*Pause.*] Dearest Ruth.

RUTH: Since I slept on my own I've been so *afraid*. So
afraid of violent *black* — [*A gush.*] Oh please
don't let's go to Africa.

REUBEN: We must.

RUTH: Why?

REUBEN: [*confession*] Because I promised — I promised
your sister when I knew her in this bed.

> [RUTH *is stunned.*]

I made love to her. I went up looking for the
source of noise and — *twice* . . . [*Pause.*] I can
see no bottom to the depths of my moral turpi-

tude. With your kind permission, I shall shoot myself.

> [RUTH *weeps on the bed, with a frenzied gnashing of teeth.*]

RUTH: You did it to spite me! To get out of this! *She* did it to spite me!

> [*She takes the whole bottle of chloral, rather messily.*]

You beast — don't you dare use force on me — you will only take me when I am *dead!*

> [*She tears open her dress at the front.*]

When I am *dead!*

> [*She falls back unconscious.* REUBEN *produces a farewell note quickly, gets out a revolver, and shoots himself without more ado through the temple. He falls over with the blast behind the bed. He sits up again.*]

REUBEN: [*weakly*] I can't see . . . Is there anybody there . . .? anybody there . . .?

> [*The light starts to fade on that scene. The* VAMPIRE *comes in, dressed and cowled in black, and carries off* RUTH. REUBEN *whimpers on the floor.*]
>
> [*The light dies completely.*]
>
> [*The light comes up on the other side of the stage.* DAVIS *is holding the suicide note. He is in the process of banishing* JOY. *He points the way.*]

DAVIS: Traitress! Whore! Jezebel! Never darken my doorway again! Get you to Babylon where you belong!

> [*They tableau in a position of banisher and banished. Through the*

> *tableau a figure in evening dress appears. He walks into a spot and the tableau light dies. It is* CHARLES DICKENS, *with a reading script.*]

DICKENS: My name, as you probably know, is Charles Dickens. I used to do lecture tours, reading my own work. I had to see them laugh. I had to see them weep. Yes, weep, for the death of innocence, for the death of a child. I am going to read to you tonight from that favourite piece of mine in the *Old Curiosity Shop*. The death of little Nell, in the North Midlands, after her flight from the terrors of London with her grandfather and, at the home of a friendly poor school-teacher, she . . .

> *[He is overcome by emotion and stops; he produces a large red and white spotted handkerchief.]*

She . . . it was — snowing . . .

> *[A passing bell starts to toll, mournfully.]*

She . . . you see, she . . .

> *[He is overcome again. Berlioz' Requiem begins to swell in the background. He lets out a stupendous cry of grief, of unimaginable magnitude.]*

Aaaaaaaaaaaugh!

> *[He exits.]*

ACT ONE: Scene Two

Characters

MRS SUGG   *Seance room proprietress*
REUBEN
AL FUNG   *A Chinese photographer*
DAVIS
JOY
SOLDIER

SCENE TWO

Scene Two uses the whole stage area as one room — Sugg's Clairvoyant Parlour, also a brothel. REUBEN *is now blind and his personality has been transformed by his attempted suicide; he is a coarser, simpler person.* MRS SUGG, *a speedy Grande Dame, is talking to him.*

MRS SUGG: Reuben, did you get that parcel from Farringdon for me?

[JOY *comes on dressed in muslin drapes.* AL FUNG, *a Chinese photographer, poses her in erotic kitsch poses against a cloth backdrape of a suitable kind.* REUBEN *is sat down downstage, fingering a tin whistle.* MRS SUGG *turns to* JOY.]

I told him to get a parcel from Farringdon and he hasn't. This isn't a charity. [*to* REUBEN] This isn't a charity, you know.

[JOY *takes no notice.*]

Reuben, I gave you half a crown to get a C.O.D. parcel for me from Farringdon railway station and you haven't been, have you?

REUBEN: Well, no.

MRS SUGG: Why not! D'you want to end up begging on the street?

REUBEN: No —

[*He starts playing* I know that my Redeemer liveth.]

MRS SUGG: Well you will! If you carry on like this, I'll kick you out dearie. I'm sorry but I can't have passengers.

REUBEN: Joy, my spiritual sister will not desert me in the valley of the shadow.

MRS SUGG: And I don't care if she goes too! There are plenty more where you two came from [*contemptuously*] Wales! And that bloody tune's getting on my nerves!

JOY: Mrs Sugg, I don't fancy whoring.

MRS SUGG: Delicately put, dearie, but tonight I'm just asking you to do the seance . . .

JOY: Not ever.

MRS SUGG: All right dearie, we'll see, but there's many a finer girl who's had to put her legs in the air for a living before now. All right, just the seance for now. But later, you've got Reuben to feed — we'll see. [*to* REUBEN] Can you play anything else?

REUBEN: [*with sudden dignity*] Madam, in my time, the flageolet, the serpent, the piccolo, fiddle, and once, the harmonium for a funeral.

MRS SUGG: Just play *Yankee Doodle*. [*to* JOY] That's better, dearie.

> [*She exits.* REUBEN *carries on playing* I know that my Redeemer liveth. JOY *concludes with* AL FUNG.]

REUBEN: Joy, after the seance will you take me for a walk?

JOY: Where?

REUBEN: I want to go to the estuary. Remember how I used to collect fossils? I want to see what they're like here.

JOY: It's filthy, in the river. Everything's dead.

> [*She leads him off.*]

REUBEN: I don't mind.

> [AL FUNG *exits.* MRS SUGG *comes in and shouts at them as they retreat.*]

MRS SUGG: Hurry up, there's a clergyman banging on the door, he'll have it down quick as kiss your hand — Joy — hurry up and change for the seance — and watch out dearie, there's a nasty rat in the passage, should make you all the quicker, just the thought of it . . .

> [*She exits on the trot again.* DAVIS *enters by himself and hesitantly sits at the table. He practises transferring his hands from praying to the seance position.* REUBEN *and* AL FUNG *are putting things away, producing the coffin from backstage. As they lay it on the bed the* SOLDIER *appears.* AL FUNG *disappears; the* SOLDIER *raps on the coffin with his knuckles and then climbs in.*]

REUBEN: You can't get in the coffin — it's for the medium —

SOLDIER: I haven't done it in a coffin before. I had . . . [*a steely manic mumble*] . . . twenty virgins last year and I did *It*. I like 'em small. I had to kill two of them to stop them screaming, the lying little bastards. When I did *It*. One for the left, one for the right, and I kissed their little golden curls all through the night.

REUBEN: Excuse me, sir . . .

SOLDIER: You know where you are with little girls.

REUBEN: [*calling*] Mrs Sugg! We got a rum one here . . .

> [MRS SUGG *enters and passes the table.* DAVIS *clutches at her and holds her.*]

DAVIS: I am the curate of a small parish in Carmarthenshire. My wife drowned whilst bathing in the sea. One of my daughters went mad and vanished and another killed herself on her wedding night and the last one died in a cholera epidemic.

SOLDIER: Lolling about in doorways ... reek of muff round rotten stairs ...

DAVIS: [*still clutching at* MRS SUGG] It's not a lapse in faith ... I just want to see if there's anything behind the veil — with modern scientific advances ...

> [REUBEN *has dashed across to* MRS SUGG *and is holding her from the other side.*]

REUBEN: He'll kill us all! He's off his head!

DAVIS: It's grief ...

MRS SUGG: Thank you.

> [*Disentangling herself from them both, she pushes* REUBEN *out.*]

DAVIS: [*at the table, almost to himself*] I don't want this to be known — do you think God will damn me because the church was too poor to afford a governess ...?

SOLDIER: I want *It* in here.

MRS SUGG: [*to the* SOLDIER] If you can just hang on till this gentleman has finished — but you can't stay in there — Thursday night's seance night — but just hang on for half an hour ...

> [*She drags the* SOLDIER *out and over to the table.*]

You sit there where I can keep an eye on you.

> [*They all sit.*]

DAVIS: [*to them both*] I looked and I looked, I couldn't see her anywhere — probably dead of starvation or typhus or filthy, slackmouthed and abandoned, round Charing Cross, not able to remember her name ... They said about my

wife that it was suicide. I wanted to give her a
Christian burial but there was a strong argu-
ment amongst the deacons for putting her outside of sacred ground altogether. I would like
to ask God if he knows what he's doing ...

MRS SUGG: We of the Sugg Clairvoyant Parlour ...

DAVIS: Oh God. We ask Thy blessing in this quest for
loved ones lost who are, perhaps, heedless in a
different place ...

MRS SUGG: Amen. Gentlemen ... [*She claps her hands.*]
Gentlemen, we are ready. I would like to assure
you no mechanical devices are used and no
tricks of the eye to deceive the intelligence or
credibility. Whatever you see will be strictly
true. You may, if you like, examine the fur-
niture for hollow legs, mirrors, springs, boxes,
partitions and objects glued to the under-
surface.

DAVIS: Now I'm sure that —

MRS SUGG: [*ploughing on without stopping*] You will
find none of them. However, once the seance
has started you are expressly forbidden to
touch anything unless the spirit asks you. You
may be responsible for bringing the medium
out of her trance at a point where she will leave
her sanity behind. In the meantime, however,
you may examine the stuffing of the chairs
before we start, the antimacassars, in the parrot
cage, behind the Crown Derby, under the
fender, in the curtain lining, the atmospheric
clock, the mahogany hatstand, the Indian
carpet, the brass drop hinges, the gas lights, the
bell pull and the counterweight recesses in the
sash windows. You are requested by the

management not to probe the ceiling below as it is leased to a loan company separate from this enterprise, or the floor above, as we have had complaints from the seamstresses there of penknife blades trying to force the tongue and groove flooring apart. This is trespass and they have threatened to call the police if it happens again.

[*She ushers them round the table.*]
I would like in advance half a guinea from each of you to defray the costs of the performance and the hire of the room. This is the only performance today: nothing will be held back.

[*She goes round collecting money.*]
The medium, Miss Kersalone, cannot perform more than once a day because of the strain on her psychic faculties.

[JOY *sweeps in swathed in white muslin and lies in the coffin.*]
Miss Kersalone is here now. I would remind you that she has triumphantly toured America. If you wish you may examine her box before we start.

[*The lights go down even further.*]
Keep your knees well down from the underside of the table and place the tips of the fingers against the surface. Remember that the communicants come from the other world and do not press your worldly wisdom of judgement on them too hard. They may be withholding knowledge which they know is best for you to be in ignorance of, that is painful or injurious. The management accepts no

responsibility for hats, coats and personal possessions which may be removed to the other side. The bodies you see are astral. You cannot buy them.

> [*The lights are now off. Pause. A small bell tinkles.*]

She is ready.

> [*Pause.*]

Where are we?

JOY: [*in a weak, heavy voice*] I'm here.

MRS SUGG: Where are we?

JOY: [*in the same voice*] Jerusalem ...

SOLDIER: That was quick.

> [*Shushings by* MRS SUGG.]

DAVIS: [*querulously*] I have come to talk to Joy, Jesse, Ruth, Margaret ...

MRS SUGG: Take what is here and be thankful!

> [*Faintly, the sound of cicadas. Distant voices, inaudible. A steam train's whistle and the noise of shunting in the distance. Then, very close, the braying of an ass.*]

SOLDIER: I say, that was a bit close.

MRS SUGG: Once more and you're out.

> [*Pause.*]

JOY: We do, oh we *do*, oh we *do*, oh we *do*, oh we *do*, oh we *do*, oh ...

> [*Pause.*]

MRS SUGG: Is there anybody there?

> [*Creaking and groaning and knocking. A ship's siren.*]

Where are we now?

> [JOY *giggles stupidly.*]

JOY: [*in the same voice*] Jerusalem ...

DAVIS: It's going to blaspheme! It's going to curse God!

MRS SUGG: Quiet! [*Pause.*] Where are you now?
[*Pause.*]

JOY: [*with sudden monstrous violence*] Entirely monstrous and inhuman noises in perpetual recurrence — wild bellowing and howling — obscene wretches in the night — clashing of church bells reaching for miles into the quiet air — every word a mean passion or unclean jest . . .
[*Pause.*]

MRS SUGG: Where are you now?

JOY: [*in the old voice*] Jerusalem.

MRS SUGG: What do you see?

JOY: The Negro . . . and his haunting, melancholy music . . . the descent to death . . . flight from fear, and want . . . hunger . . . away from the eternal struggle against suffering and oppression . . . America.
[*A flute plays* Yankee doodle, *live.* AL FUNG *carries an American flag round the table.* REUBEN *is dimly visible playing the flute.* JOY *gets out of the coffin and goes behind the bathing machine.* AL FUNG *draws the drapes off the bathing machine.*]

DAVIS: What has this got to do with me?

MRS SUGG: That mad one may have gone to America.

DAVIS: [*piqued*] Well, I want to see a sign.
[*At the same time,* JOY *appears in the doorway of the bathing hut, which is lit at a low light.*]

MRS SUGG: You will see your little ones. Hold your little ones.

[*A puff of flame and smoke.* JOY *is lit
in front of the bathing machine.*]

JOY: Jerusalem . . .

DAVIS: [*unbelieving*] It's my wife — transformed to
Heavenly glory. Margaret —
[*He rushes to the bathing hut and
seizes her. She flees behind.*]

JOY: Ow!

MRS SUGG: Quick, Al Fung, cover up the hut.

SOLDIER: I saw that! I heard that!

MRS SUGG: One of the clients has interrupted the vision.
The seance must come to an end . . .
[JOY *flees from behind the bathing
machine and jumps into the coffin.*
DAVIS *hotly pursues her and jumps in
after her.*]

DAVIS: My love — you're so young again . . .

MRS SUGG: Get them out — Reuben —
[REUBEN *throws out the* SOLDIER. *The
lights are still murky.* DAVIS *is still
trying to make it in the coffin.*]

DAVIS: [*taking off his trousers*] Away! Away with
earthly trousers!

MRS SUGG: Al Fung — quick — get the camera — we'll
make him pay for this.

JOY: Mrs Sugg, his breath smells!

MRS SUGG: Never mind, dearie, we'll make it worth your
while . . .
[AL FUNG *is setting up the camera.*]

AL FUNG: Get some flash powder — Reuben . . .
[*They take the photograph in great
haste.* AL FUNG *goes off behind the
bathing machine. The* SOLDIER
returns by himself.]

SOLDIER: I want my money back.

MRS SUGG: No.

SOLDIER: Or a turn with her.

MRS SUGG: No.

> [*The* SOLDIER *produces a knife.*]

Put that away. We are civilised people.

> [*Pause. She employs a different tack.*]

If you use force I shall invoke Beelzebub.

DAVIS: No ... no ...

> [*He is still embracing* JOY *and trying to get her muslin drapes off.*]

If you do that you take away my heaven ...

> [*The* SOLDIER *goes to* DAVIS *and puts the knife under his throat.*]

SOLDIER: Out.

MRS SUGG: Beelzebub!

> [AL FUNG *appears with a black drape round him and spits petrol in the* SOLDIER'S *face.* REUBEN *lights a match far too late and too far away. The* SOLDIER *lashes out blindly at* AL FUNG *with the knife and stabs him.* AL FUNG *dies.*]

REUBEN: [*not realising what has happened*] Ho ho ho, with my fiery breath, I'll burn you down ...

> [*He finds* AL FUNG *on the floor.*]

SOLDIER: It's a devil is it!

REUBEN: He's all wet, Mrs Sugg ... He's dead ...

MRS SUGG: [*to the* SOLDIER] Stop! You have just killed a man.

> [*The* SOLDIER *is trying to pull* DAVIS *off* JOY *in the coffin.*]

SOLDIER: I'm going to kill a woman now ... roll her in the Chink's blood ... entrails ... pretty patterns on the floor ... rip ... and rip ...

[*He takes off his tunic.*]
Mustn't get that dirty, now ...

[*The resourceful* MRS SUGG *produces a Colt .45, which has been strapped to her inner thigh. She points the gun unsteadily at the* SOLDIER. *(NB: It is essential to have a proper gun with a loud report. There is no such thing as a melodramatic starting pistol.)*]

MRS SUGG: It won't go off!

JOY: [*from underneath*] Try the safety catch!

[MRS SUGG *releases the safety catch and fires, killing* DAVIS. REUBEN *rushes out from the bathing hut, brandishing a stick in all directions.*]

REUBEN: Don't make a move, any of you! One more step and you're dead!

[*He comes between* MRS SUGG *and the* SOLDIER *just as* MRS SUGG *is firing again.* REUBEN *goes down.*]

Oh noble six hundred!

[*The* SOLDIER *now advances on* MRS SUGG *as it appears there is no movement from the coffin.*]

SOLDIER: Rip ... and rip ... and rip ...

[MRS SUGG *has blown her cool and fails to fire, the last two times having been disastrous. The* SOLDIER *seizes her gun arm and she drops the gun. The* SOLDIER *starts stabbing her in the stomach, up against the piano.*]

SOLDIER: Rip ... and rip ... and rip ...

[JOY *pushes her father off her to see what is happening.*]

JOY: [*recognising* DAVIS *as he falls to the floor*] Father!

> [MRS SUGG *groans horribly.* JOY *sees what is happening and goes over and picks up the revolver and fires it, killing the* SOLDIER. *He slides to the floor.* MRS SUGG *staggers over to the piano and sits down.*]

MRS SUGG: Do you *know* any of these people?

JOY: One was my father ...

> [REUBEN'*s blind spectacles have fallen off on the floor. She recognises him.*]

The other was my lover ...

MRS SUGG: Very young for your father — oh, I see, that one ... still, times change ... Look, they'll think it's a family quarrel and they're bound to hang you for it — so what I should do is to get into the Hussar's uniform and hit the street — take my purse ...

> [JOY *rapidly changes.* REUBEN *is thrashing around on the floor and meets up with* DAVIS. *They are both dying. Distantly, on record,* I know that my Redeemer liveth *starts.*]

REUBEN: My name is Reuben Mavros, from Aberdovey. From there, I have come to the river, the estuary. Blue clay here, embedded in which the fossils of animals which prove ... once I was a vigorous amateur paleo —

DAVIS: Reuben ...! I'm your father-in-law ...

REUBEN: Faith is a ... great comfort in death ... we belong to the ... true faith ... the revived church ...

DAVIS: Yes ... and I shall see my wife again, and *again* ...

REUBEN: And I can see castles ... and glory ...

DAVIS: It'll do.

[*He dies.* JOY *kisses all three good-bye.*]

JOY: Goodbye, father, goodbye Reuben, goodbye Mrs Sugg.

MRS SUGG: Good luck, dearie.

[JOY *slips off.* MRS SUGG *looks round from the piano stool, and dies as the music swells.*]

[*Fade to blackout.*]

END OF ACT ONE

ACT TWO

Characters

ANTHEA
SARAH
VIOLET
HENRY TIETZENS   *Anthea's fiancé*
JUNG
FREUD
OX
JOSEPH
MARY

> SARAH, VIOLET *and* ANTHEA *are standing mid-stage watching a cricket match. They wear big Edwardian dresses.* SARAH *has a dog: a small one on a lead. The other two have parasols. Small business for a few seconds. The sound of outdoor clapping, scattered.* VIOLET *looks away from the match (off-stage left) and then back again.* ANTHEA *sniffs a rose, wipes her nose and puts the handkerchief back in her sleeve.*

ANTHEA: Oh! [*She turns away from the match.*] He's dropped it.
> [*Pause. Scattered applause again.*]

SARAH: No he hasn't.
> [*Pause.*]
Didn't Henry used to open?

ANTHEA: He's terribly off form. Henry . . .
> [*Scattered applause.*]
When Daddy went to Tibet with the regiment, he met an old man in a pass who said, 'What is the sound of one hand clapping?' [*Pause.*] Stupid old man.

SARAH: When was he there?

ANTHEA: Ten or twelve years ago — just after the Queen died.
> [HENRY TIETZENS *appears, ready to go in.*]

HENRY: [*facetiously*] Good afternoon, Miss Fox, Lambert and Stephen-Bailey.

SARAH: Come and talk to us, Henry.

HENRY: Not if Violet's wearing her suffragette colours.

ANTHEA: She's not — she's meeting her mother for tea.

HENRY: [*still at a distance*] What a horrid little dog that is.

SARAH: Don't you dare say that, you beast.
[*She picks it up and holds it to her.*]

HENRY: Is that the one that's always bringing up its lunch?

SARAH: No. That's a German dog.

HENRY: Did you know I was related to Bismarck?

ANTHEA: When the war starts, Henry, you and the dog can go and fight on the other side.

SARAH: [*to the dog*] Bite him. Bite him.

HENRY: I'll see you all later. Bye bye Anthea.
[*He exits.*]

VIOLET: [*to* SARAH] Didn't your mother have her eye on him at one time?

SARAH: [*absently*] Yes, but then she's a silly gel. [*to the dog*] Bite him! Bite him!

ANTHEA: Is it breeding?

SARAH: What — my mother or the dog?

VIOLET: I want to hear about your mother, and she wants to hear about the dog.

SARAH: Well, the dog's coming into season in a few weeks but mother's been off it for some time —
[VIOLET *and* ANTHEA *both laugh.*]
There's been incest.

ANTHEA: [*absentmindedly*] You can't really guard against it if you bring up a litter — they don't know any better when the bitch goes on heat . . .

SARAH: [*to* VIOLET] My *grandmother* and my great grandfather, during a seance, in a coffin, and before that in a bathing machine.

ANTHEA: Good God. Where! I'm sorry I mentioned it.

VIOLET: [*to* SARAH] Oh — come . . .

SARAH: All the witnesses including her lover were killed.

ANTHEA: Oh really . . . I mean, oh, *really* . . . I don't

believe it.

VIOLET: I don't know, it sounds Victorian . . . terribly so . . .

ANTHEA: They weren't like that at all. I can't believe that . . .

SARAH: She swears it's true. She's dead now. He was a Welsh clergyman.

ANTHEA: Nonsense. [*She is watching the game.*] Oh. Oh! He's fallen over.
[*She turns away.*]

VIOLET: Who?

ANTHEA: I can't see without my glasses.

VIOLET: Was it rape?

SARAH: She did used to say . . . 'There is no rape, there is only the wrong man.'

VIOLET: And your grandfather?

SARAH: Killed by a stray bullet during conception. They do say, it brings it on . . .

ANTHEA: But why a seance?

SARAH: Feelings ran very high in those days.
[*They all nod sagely.*]

ANTHEA: They musta . . .
[SARAH *suddenly starts to laugh.*]

SARAH: It was an easy mistake to make in the dark — but my grandmother, who escaped from the scene in a Hussar's uniform, was picked up and had to do the most horrible things with an officer she met in the Strand just afterwards . . .
[*Neither of the other two think that it's funny.* SARAH *continues to laugh.*]

VIOLET: Henry's in the Hussars, isn't he?

ANTHEA: Yes.

SARAH: She did cover herself, though. She married money.

ANTHEA: We're all keen to do that, dear.

[*Pause.*]

There's nothing wrong with Henry.

[*Pause.*]

SARAH: [*mischievously*] Except he's so poor ...

ANTHEA: He's got family money!

VIOLET: Stop bitching, you two.

[HENRY *is carried through with a star-burst of blood on his forehead, by two attendants. The three girls turn.*]

CARRIER 1: He wasn't looking.

CARRIER 2: Idiot ...

[*They go off.*]

SARAH: He must have been looking at you, Anthea.

ANTHEA: It is a brutishly dull game, certainly.

SARAH: Are you sure he gets an allowance?

ANTHEA: Nothing to go to town on. Poor Henry. I do hope he's all right.

VIOLET: He'll get more if there's a war.

ANTHEA: My dear girl, he'll be away if there's a war.

SARAH: Why does your mother keep giving me those piercing looks?

ANTHEA: Probably [*savagely*] because she's going blind.

VIOLET: In fact she's so blind that she thinks that Henry's handsome, and has so-called prospects.

SARAH: Anthea — really — neither mother nor I are in the least bit interested in Henry. [*Pause.*] He said ... [*She laughs.*] ... He's so funny — He said ...

[CARRIER 1 *enters.*]

CARRIER 1: Miss Stephen-Bailey?

ANTHEA: Yes.

CARRIER 1: I'm so sorry about this. I'm the Busker's team captain.

[*They shake hands.*]

ANTHEA: Is he all right?

CARRIER 1: Oh yes — he's just lying down for ten minutes ... He sent you this.

[*He gives her a folded card.* ANTHEA *reads it.*]

ANTHEA: Tell him: 'Mais oui, mon cheri.'

CARRIER 1: [*exiting*] Mais oui, mon cheri ...

VIOLET: He wants to marry you.

ANTHEA: Oh — Henry.

[*She turns away from the other two and exits after the* CARRIER.]

VIOLET: They'll be very happy together.

[SARAH *laughs.*]

He's so stupid — He said to me: 'I don't know much about this war business, but the regiment's got twenty dozen of champagne well crated, and the hounds are in fine fettle.'

[*They start to go off.*]

Won't your mother be annoyed?

SARAH: Mais oui, mon cheri.

[*Blackout.*]

[*Suddenly there is the sound of summer thunder. Spotlight on* ANTHEA *on the podium used by* CHARLES DICKENS. *She has a black arm band on and a black hat. She addresses the audience. There is a Union Jack behind her.*]

ANTHEA: Women ... [*Pause.*] ... of England ... [*Pause.*] Women ... of England. How proud I feel, and happy, to be able to address you here by that title tonight. The war has called us all to larger purposes. How we must rejoice that it has lifted us above the petty squabbles of those who want us to have votes, or property, or custody of children. In a decent world, we don't need them threatening the sanctity of motherhood! We do have an identity. It is a glorious identity. All through the last two summers, those of us who have lived in the south of our country, from Whitstable to Bournemouth and on the Weald of Kent, have heard, lying in our beds or on quiet summer evenings, the distant thunder of bombardment as the Huns, or more recently our boys, launch an offensive or counter-offensive. And we ask ourselves, how can we help? How strange, how simple and yet somehow how glorious it is to be called. We are blessed in having found a cause which stretches across geographical boundaries and the barriers of class. We must see — that that front has enough men and supplies to fight with! To bring this war to a swift end with the ignominious surrender of the Bosch! Now God be thanked that waked us at this hour! Those guns. Those ever present guns. Eighty-eights. Whizz-bangs. None of us need to be reminded of the names. They are an ever present reminder that we, our whole country, our whole way of life — is at stake! If we listen for a moment we can hear them even now.

[*She bows her head, listening reverently. Silence. She raises her head again.*]

[*bravely*] I hope you will allow me one personal anecdote. Something which after a month still touches me very deeply, and for me at least means that there can be no going back. My husband, Henry Tietzens, while leading a platoon of Hussars out of a wood in Passchendaele, was struck on the head by a shell fragment. His men gallantly carried him back. But he never recovered consciousness. Now you all know that our government has not yet brought in conscription of recruits for the front. And when you look at our soldiers and the job they have to do it is indeed a tribute to the menfolk of this country. But there is only one way to bring this struggle to an end. [*A furious climax.*] There are *men*, so called, living in this country and enjoying its protection, who have not yet offered their services. We — will never vote for conscription. We are not entitled to, we do not wish to. And yet we find them contemptible, these cowards. I say we should take up and redouble our efforts to send *white feathers* to shame these skulking brutes into some sense of *duty* for their country! And send them to the front to kill Germans, not to play games with them!

> [*Heroic music. Cross fade the spot to the back of the stage.* HENRY TIETZENS, *with a completely white skin, is standing in his cricket gear. He has a small starburst of blood on his whitened forehead. He carries a picture frame of gilt with a photograph in it.*]

ANTHEA: [*in the dark*] Women of England — say — 'Go! We don't want to lose you but we think you ought to — Go!'

> [*The other pool lights.* SARAH *is stand-*

*ing in it, dressed in prison uniform.
She speaks in a deadpan voice.*]

SARAH: They took me prisoner because I listened to my suffragette friends. I set fire to churches. Big churches. During the war suffragettes were forgotten or reviled. My sinuses were crushed through force-feeding. Nobody came to see me. When Henry died, *he* came to see me. He took me in my astral body to a field in Norfolk. There were buttercups.

[HENRY *goes over to* SARAH. *He bends down and kisses her neck.*]

[*lifting him off her*] Henry . . . They can see us from the pavilion.

[*She takes his hand and takes the glove off. Underneath, it is white too.*]

You'll die in bed at ninety-four with your grandchildren all around you . . . Did you know Violet wants to carry your child . . .? Or . . . anybody else's child . . .

[HENRY *sighs windily. He reaches out with one hand and starts to undress her. The other hand holds the picture still. They are both standing up.*]

Henry . . . we can be seen from the pavilion . . . It's not that I don't want to — it's just that it goes against the grain rather — *devant les autres* . . . the strain has made you antisocial . . . you've been away too long. I suppose it must be horrid out there. The noise, the people . . .

[HENRY *continues to undress her.*]

Couldn't we please move into the wood, Henry . . .? It'd be so much less of a spectacle . . . I'm rather shy, not very much of a sexual athlete . . .

HENRY: [*windily*] Football . . .

SARAH: [*stepping out of her clothes*] If you must have the rest of my clothes off — I wish we could move from the pavilion . . .

> [*They do not move. She stands naked.* HENRY *tries to show her his picture, but his hands are clumsy.*]

HENRY: Football . . .

SARAH: When you played with your cousins? In Baden-Baden? Baden-Baden for your holidays — holidays . . . [*She laughs.*]

HENRY: Foo- . . . *ball.*

SARAH: Is it true the Angels of Mons started as a newspaper story? When your wife tours the country — ten per cent of the audience have joined up within a quarter of an hour of her finishing speaking in the hall — [*She embraces him lightly.*] Hurry up, Henry, I'm getting cold . . .

> [*The picture gets in the way.* HENRY *tries to show it to her. Thus, finally, she looks at it.*]

Oh, soldiers. They *will* march in lines against machine guns. How are your men? I understand they complain of the creeping barrage. But you can always get fresh . . . fresh men from Clerkenwell. [*She looks again at the picture.*] Oh, what fun. You're playing football. And there you are — that's you — nice — Christmas 1914. [*blandly*] And the other side appears to be — Germans . . . ?

HENRY: [*raising his finger to his lips*] Ssssh!

> [HENRY *beckons with his head. He leads* SARAH *off by the hand. There is*

the sound of a wind; then the music of Silent Night. SARAH *returns with* JOSEPH *and the* OX, *as* MARY. *They move into position and tableau. Simple Passion Play clothes. Pause. The* OX *swiftly pinches* MARY's *arse. She titters. There is a roll of thunder and the stage darkens.* FREUD *arrives at the back of the stage.*]

MARY: [*kittenish*] Is there anyone there?

FREUD: [*in a voice like granite and ashes*] My name is Sigmund Freud. Originally, all of the dead were vampires. They had a grudge against the living and sought to injure them and rob them of their lives. We fear the dead because we fear death still and wish to put off what must be the gravest misfortune. [*He paces uneasily.*] Our bodies, however, are destined to decay and cannot dispense with anxiety and pain as warning signals. There is no escape. We are told that —

MARY: Can't you just *imagine* you're happy?

FREUD: We are told that in certain regions of the earth where nature provides in abundance there are races who do not know coercion and whose lives are passed in tranquillity. *Ha!*

MARY: But Mr Freud . . .

FREUD: I can scarcely believe it. I would be glad to hear more of these fortunate beings. My life has been a little island of pain in the great sea of unconsciousness. [*modestly*] Just like anybody else.

MARY: But when you were a child —

FREUD: Little children . . . sadists and animal torturers

may evolve into sentimentalists and friends of
humanity but they can never be free of their
original impulses and the anguish of arrested
desire. Beat. Bite. Fuck. Kill. Terror.

> [*Pause. Thunder.* JUNG *emerges into
> the nativity tableau. He is dressed in a
> white coat. He looks like Dr. Kildare.
> He has a doctor's bag. He goes to*
> MARY *and looks over her to the
> audience.*]

JUNG: [*to the audience*] My name is Dr Carl Jung.

MARY: [*getting his attention*] Oh, doctor, doctor ...
I've been having these dreams ...

JUNG: [*to the audience*] There is a charming tradition
mentioned by the English poet Hardy that the
animals are freed from their beastly dumbness
for the duration of Christmas and are able to
talk, simultaneous to the virgin birth —

> [*He tries to examine* MARY *but she
> darts away.*]

OX: [*sotto voce, breathy*] Let's go to my place and
fuck.

JOSEPH: [*very open, to the audience*] I was by myself in
the Adriatic — no — I was bending down to
feed the rabbits — he didn't even introduce
himself ...

OX: Let's go to my pool and fuck.

MARY: I wasn't married at the time — didn't know
anything about it — I'm sure I was feeding the
rabbits ... [*a different idea*] I was at the panto-
mime — a man stood up on a ladder and made
a funny noise — it was then! [*She blows an ex-
panding whistle.*] And the Angel of the Lord in
the sky and he said: 'Don't you worry, because

you're going to have a baby — and everything's going to be all right!' [*Pause.*] I didn't know what to say — He said I'd only fallen to earth, not hurt myself ...

OX: [*with arrested desire*] Aaahh ...

MARY: I did feel *hands* sometimes ... going up my skirt ... but always in funny places — speedboats — carnivals — I didn't say anything at the time ... I thought I was imagining — I had to pinch myself to find out if it was real —!

> [*Long pause. The* OX *turns to the audience.*]

OX: [*sotto voce rumble*] I was ... in the manger when it was born, I was ... Three men come in off of a flying saucer in leather coats and put something there instead of it. They told me to keep quiet about it ... What they put down looked like lots of things but, mostly, like a little *pudd'n* ...

> [*Pause.*]

FREUD: Many will find it hard to abandon belief that in man there dwells an impulse to perfection that has brought him this far. I do not believe it. I see no way of preserving this pleasing illusion.

OX: [*thoughtfully*] Pudd'n ...

MARY: [*to* JUNG] Oh, doctor, doctor ...

JUNG: [*soothing*] What Freud has to say can be taken as the truest expression of his own, personal psychology. But there are no misunderstandings in nature, any more than the fact that the earth only has one moon is a misunderstanding. In this story there is the earth, the moon and the sun.

MARY: Was it in the wind when I bent down to pick up

the washing? Will it hurt?

[*She prepares to give birth.*]

FREUD: At one time or another, by some operation of force which still baffles conjecture, the properties of life were awakened in lifeless matter . . .

OX: Pudd'n . . .

JUNG: [*spreading a white sheet over* MARY] The earth in one form is a maiden, held prisoner by the winter, covered in ice and snow . . . the young spring sun, the fiery hero melts her out of her frosty prisoner where she has long awaited her delivery and she gives forth fruit.

> [JUNG *produces a baby from underneath the white sheet. It is bright red. It has hideous fangs protruding out of its mouth like a vampire. It is quite revolting. He holds it up with great, smug pride, away from* MARY *and speaks to the audience as if he were advertising detergent, without looking at it.*]

For thousands of years rites of initiation have been teaching rebirth from the spirit, and yet man forgets again and again the meaning of divine procreation. The penalty for misunderstanding is — neurotic decay, embitterment, and sterility. But there are human beings who *understand* that God is their father and so . . . history repeats itself.

> [*He hands the baby to* MARY. HENRY *and the* OX *go and get the coffin and bring it on. Inside there is a stake and a mallet.*]

FREUD: Dead men . . . women menstruating or in

labour ... the fact that they are helpless is bound to give the survivors encouragement to give vent to their hostile passions.

[FREUD *slowly gets into the coffin.* HENRY *slowly lowers the lid as* FREUD *continues to talk.*]

Happiness is the problem of balancing the economics of the libido of the personality. Suffering comes from three quarters, from our bodies, which are destined to decay and cannot dispense with anxiety and pain as danger signals, from the outer world, which can rage against us with the most powerful and pitiless forces of destruction, and finally from our relationships with other men — we are inclined ...

[*By this time the* OX *and* HENRY *are about to bash in the stake. They give it one tap and it goes through the lid.* FREUD *stops talking. They bash the stake into his heart. It takes a long time.* FREUD *beats on the coffin, trying to get out, then subsides. Finally they stop and stand up as the stake reaches the other side of the coffin.* JOSEPH *and* MARY *and the teeny Vampire baby exit hurriedly in a state of shock.* JUNG *has watched it all.* Silent Night *starts again, very faintly.*]

OX: [*proprietorial*] Well, whaddya know.

[HENRY *and the* OX *turn to go.*]

JUNG: [*interested*] What *do* you know?

OX: [*exiting*] Nothing. But I know it good.

ACT THREE

Characters

ROLAND
JAMES
DWIGHT
JILL
MOIRA
MAN

Author's Note

The original last 'Vampire' was not unalike Enoch Powell, but satire ages quickly and is often local, so the figure has changed from the Ayatollah Khomeini, to Colonel Kentucky, depending on the news of the day. I had hoped to find a permanent vampire but that is contradicted by the structure of the play. The speech adapts well enough to different speakers with a little tailoring.

Very faintly and distantly, the Rolling Stones: Gimme Shelter. It is dark. A slow light from behind a ragged curtain, which partly covers an attic window. We gradually see two figures asleep on a mattress on the floor. They are bikers. Next to them is a coffin with the lid off. The music grows with the light. Both take their time. The two bikers slowly awaken and get up. They put on their gear. One of them sniffs at the body in the coffin and wrinkles his nose. The other shakes his head, disapprovingly, and puts down the lid. They are now dressed in their leathers after some minutes, and after flexing their shoulders, at an agreed signal, they pick up the coffin and exit with it, swiftly and easily.

Blackout the faint light. Bring up the music for the change. Cut the music and snap on all the lights ...

MOIRA, JILL *and* DWIGHT *are talking midstage.* MOIRA *and* JILL *are two reporters. They are all heavily confectioned but* DWIGHT *steals the show. She has platform heels, a red wig, split ciré skirt, and highly rouged cheekbones. The other two are simply colourfully dressed. Everybody is wearing a lot of make-up. Otherwise, a bare stage.*

JILL: Marcia —
DWIGHT: Dwight.
JILL: Sorry?
DWIGHT: Dwight. Dwight now.

JILL: Why Dwight?

MOIRA: I think it's a lovely name.

DWIGHT: It's a horrid name but he was a lovely general.

MOIRA: Why not Patton?

DWIGHT: Because he was a shit-eating fascist.

JILL: D'you want to make this formal or informal?

DWIGHT: Oh — utterly formal — pretend you know nothing about me — indecent past and wicked future — [*She laughs.*]

JILL: You've changed a great deal since —

DWIGHT: I adore change — I want to have a gallery, you know, with different coloured lights, on time switches, constantly changing. I do feel older, but not subjectively — only intuitively — after all, compared to precious metals or rocks, I'm terribly young — that goes even for the sort of rocks you get off —

[*She gives a dazzling smile.*]

JILL: You used to be a great advocate of homosexual marriage.

DWIGHT: Right now I think that love is more important. You see, there's a long tradition of free thinking in my family — my grandmother got laid by somebody — posthumously — that's why I think it would be such a good idea to start a sperm bank — you could have anyone you want — her grandmother had incest with her father ... yes, I am against regular marriage. Anyway ... I said it because I was living with this mean, ordinary person at the time — I wanted to shock the shit out of him ... boy was he obsessive about shit ... I know, now, what mean people do — they sit out their life on the lavatory with a novel in one hand

and a bowl of Complan in the other, shit and
eat at the same time — so they know they're not
losing anything . . . After a bit I said to him —
'You're not having any of this arse, baby — you
go and put that prick of yours in a turd.'

JILL: What are you doing now?

DWIGHT: I'm organising a funeral for some bikers.

JILL: I didn't know there were any left.

DWIGHT: Oh, it's like a cabal — word of mouth, father to
son . . .

MOIRA: Why are you doing that?

DWIGHT: So's I won't get bored.

JILL: Are you ever bored?

DWIGHT: No! I have a terribly exciting life. I'm one of
the least bored people alive. Loneliness and
shyness are terrible problems for a lot of
people, but they find they can talk about themselves to me, or hear me talking — little bit of
healthy narcissism never did anyone any harm
. . . Everybody's their own most exciting
person, anyhow, or ought to be. Otherwise it
becomes downright unhealthy.

JILL: What do you want to do with your life now?

DWIGHT: I want to play blues . . . I want some cornflakes
. . . and, yes, I want to start a sperm vault. Start
with your friends, deep-freeze them, and then
after they're dead, or when they become
famous, chip 'em out, flog 'em off . . . You
could have room for a million million cubes of
semen in this room . . . people would pay a
pound a year storage costs . . . Phil Spectre and
Royalty frozen free . . . of course, everybody's
famous to themselves. But not when they're
dead.

ff::

JILL: D'you believe in Heaven?

[DWIGHT *laughs.*]

DWIGHT: The answer to question twenty-three is ... Heaven is where the homosexual fascists go for a bit on the side.

[ROLAND *and* JAMES *bring on the coffin and put it on a stand in the middle of the stage.*]

[*to* JILL *and* MOIRA] Ah, shop. Don't laugh, this is business.

[ROLAND *and* JAMES *are dressed as before.* DWIGHT *proceeds to charm them with her south London guile.*]

We could have helped you up the steps with it — but it's too late now. I hope it won't embarrass you if I ask for the money in advance — 'cos my creditors are banging on the door.

[ROLAND *gives her a thick envelope. She takes it.*]

Thank you. Lovely.

[*She gives it to* MOIRA.]

Can you take whatever I owe you, love. [*addressing* ROLAND *and* JAMES] I'd like to thank you first off for choosing me. I feel flattered and happy that someone who was a great friend of us all should have friends like you who made such a tasteful choice. [*She beams.*] Sit down.

[*They sit.*]

Now of course it's pretty useless saying anything when someone dies, isn't it? I mean, we all know that there isn't anything up there. But it's us who need to get these people out of our lives, to get rid of them, to bury them. But

because death is final, it is quite *big* ...
y'know, I mean we all come to it ... and
although we're not thinking about it all the
time, it's quite a good idea at times like this to
use other people's experience who have
wanted to think about it the whole time ...
[*she gives an enchanting smile.*] So I'm going
to read to you from something which all of us
know to be untrue in the sense that we know
the poor girl's deluded ... but even if she is off
her nut, she ... wrote some quite nice stuff ...
[*She thumbs through a book.*] The autobiography of St Theresa of Lisieux. Anyone
heard of her? [*She looks up.*] Good. Terrific.
Smashing. It'll all be new then. [*She starts to
read.*] 'The time came for me to take the habit
...' [*aside to* MOIRA] No jokes, now. [*She goes
on, gradually abandoning the book.*] Nothing
was lacking, not even snow. When I was little I
used to be enchanted by its whiteness — I do
not know how it began, perhaps it was because
I was a little winter flower ... [*The book is cast
aside.*] The first sign which met my baby eyes
was the snow — like a lovely mantle, covering
the earth. But I had almost given up hope, the
day before was so warm it might have been
spring. I wanted to see nature clad like myself
in white, on my clothing day. [*The south
London accent starts to fade.*] Then the day
came and the weather was just the same so I
gave up my childish desire as impossible of
realisation, and went out to where father was
waiting for me at the cloister door. His eyes
were full of tears as he came towards me. "Here

is my little queen," he said and pressed me to his heart ... He offered me his arm and we made a breathless entry into the chapel ... It was his day of triumph, his last feast on earth. He had no more to give. His whole family belonged to God. Afterwards, the moment I set foot in the cloister, my eyes fell upon my little statue of the child Jesus smiling at me from the midst of flowers and lights — I turned away to the quadrangle — and I saw that it was — completely covered in snow! What delicacy on the part of Jesus! To gratify his little bride's every desire, he had sent her snow!

> [ROLAND *and* JAMES *start to heave and weep convulsively.*]

What mortal man could ever cause one flake to fall from the sky to charm the one he loves? The unbelievable condescension of the spouse of virgins who loves his lilies to be white as snow ... Our Lord ... made me think of the caresses he would soon be lavishing on me in front of all the saints — what consolation it brought me — and inexpressible sweetness — like the foretaste of Heavenly glory ...

> [*She pauses luxuriously.* ROLAND *and* JAMES' *sniffles subside.*]

I retired to the cell at midnight. I had not been given permission to watch all night. I had scarcely laid my head on the pillow — when I felt a burning stream rise to my lips. I restrained my curiosity and slept peacefully till the morning. The rising bell went at five o'clock — I remembered that there was some good news awaiting me! I went over to the

window and ... [*ecstatic*] It was good news —
our handkerchief was soaked in blood! I was
filled with hope — convinced that my beloved,
on the anniversary of his death, had let me hear
his first call — a far-off lovely murmur,
heralding his approach. When I was a child,
suffering made me sad, but now I taste its
bitterness with joy, and peace.

> [ROLAND *and* JAMES *clasp each other
> ecstatically and gaze to Heaven.*
> DWIGHT *goes to the piano and sits
> down. She starts to play* I know that
> my Redeemer ... *etc.* MOIRA *goes over
> and stands at the piano. The con-
> versation continues over the music.*]

MOIRA: D'you still collect pictures?
DWIGHT: [*reverting to the south London accent*] It's a
pouf's game. I gave it up.
MOIRA: That big one of a couple on a beach ...
DWIGHT: Eternal penetration with the tide out. I got
sick of it. I needed the money.
MOIRA: Who are these people?
DWIGHT: Friends of a friend.
MOIRA: Where's the friend?
DWIGHT: In the box. I was terribly fond of him.
MOIRA: He's not going to have a proper funeral?
DWIGHT: There's nothing wrong with this one, is there?
[*Pause.*] He fell off his motor-bike. [*Pause.*]
Silly boy.
MOIRA: What are you going to do now?
DWIGHT: [*irritably*] Oh — shut up a moment, will you?

> [JILL *comes over.* DWIGHT *hunches
> like a blues player but keeps playing.*]

MOIRA: Have you still got the habit?

JILL: What was she on? Dwight, what were you on?

DWIGHT: [*still playing*] Just . . . release their tensions . . they probably haven't cried in months . . . al that passion, waiting for the bomb to burst the dam.

MOIRA: You've still got the habit?

DWIGHT: No!

MOIRA: But you've sold all your paintings!

DWIGHT: I went through a phase of selling all my paintings!

MOIRA: Marcia, I don't believe you.

DWIGHT: Dwight. Believe Dwight then.

MOIRA: Can we see your arms?

DWIGHT: Uh-uh.

MOIRA: It's full of holes.

[ROLAND *and* JAMES *suddenly groan.*]

DWIGHT: I did that. And they said I was played out.

JILL: Why have you started a funeral parlour?

DWIGHT: I'm getting in on the ground floor for personalised religion. Fairy funerals feed your fabulous habit. [*Pause. The piano goes on.*] I adore religion. The Lord is my shepherd . . . [*She suddenly shouts.*] He was ugly, sulky, with a mean streak — and you threw all your passions at his feet, and he'd know what to do with your love and your hate, and they weren't expressions of you any more, they were his, and you, you were just another thought in his mind.
You loved him.
He despised you
You loved him
He ignored you.
He took you from behind with his clean

machine, and degraded your bodies. As they
should be degraded. He was the monster. And
he treated your love as it should be treated,
with utter contempt. You — will be dead to the
world when you walk the streets. Aliens.

> [ROLAND *and* JAMES *are broken up by
> this: an orgy of weeping.* DWIGHT *is
> able to continue her conversation.*]

MOIRA: There's only three days' habit in that roll.

DWIGHT: I'm on the National Health, dammit. This
hustling is just to keep me out of mischief.

MOIRA: Have you seen anything of Bill?

DWIGHT: No.

MOIRA: Do you go and see the children ever?

DWIGHT: He's having another one off the girl he's living
with now. Out of spite, presumably.

MOIRA: D'you regret leaving him?

DWIGHT: It was terrible. Toujours toujours unmade bed.
What are they doing?

> [JILL *looks at* ROLAND *and* JAMES.]

JILL: They look — oh, my God — they're not going
to open it, are they?

DWIGHT: They'll do whatever takes their fancy. Bite its
rigor mortis off for all I care . . . If you think
this is a funny end for someone, you should
hear about his brother . . .

> [ROLAND *and* JAMES *are hysterically
> clawing at the coffin but now are
> mostly exhausted.* DWIGHT *stops
> playing.*]

It's time for the largo.

> [*As she speaks the Gothic effects come
> in. The light goes down to a green spot
> on the coffin. The bell starts to toll.*]

Anyhow — his brother was called up — one of
the last people — got on the wrong train in
Berlin and was carried into Eastern Germany
. . .

> [*She laughs.* ROLAND *and* JAMES *in-*
> *dependently moan.*]

He served a sentence there — got married
twice, got drunk after having a row with the
second one and was deported with her for
making insulting remarks about the regime
. . . He got back — he could hardly speak
English — and was courtmartialled here too
. . .

> [*The Gothic effects are in full swing*
> *now.*]

I don't know about you but I think that
adequately shows the triumph of evil over
good.

> [DWIGHT, JILL *and* MOIRA *start to*
> *exit.*]

MOIRA: Perhaps you ought to ask those two to start
your sperm bank.

DWIGHT: I would, but I think they already blued it.

> [*Just the clutching hands on the coffin*
> *in the green light. The bell tolls. The*
> *hands slowly slip from the lid of the*
> *coffin. Very slowly it starts to open. A*
> *heavily cobwebbed hand emerges and*
> *grabs the side. The lid opens and the*
> *man inside sits up.*]

MAN: It often occurs in Nature that an animal is
fascinated and hypnotised by the danger which
threatens it and thus fails to escape or defend
itself while it still has the power. There is a
distinct parallel in the fate of nations: whole

peoples will watch disaster until it engulfs them, apparently unable to stir out of a horrified trance. Their will is paralysed and they cease to believe in the possibility of action. In such conditions, individuals, when they speak at all about the approaching catastrophe, are heard to say: 'It is too late, nothing will be done, nothing can be done'. You and I stand at such a place and such a time. All about me I hear it as you do, and people see with their own eyes what they dread, the transformation in their lifetime, or if they are old, in their children's, of towns, cities and areas they know into alien territory. This is the process which hundreds of thousands of our fellow citizens watch as they go about their daily business and live out their lives. And they say to themselves as they watch: 'There is no escape, this is our lot, and this will be our children's lot'. I believe there is still time once the magnitude of the danger is perceived and admitted, and I refuse to believe that the resources of the state are unequal to dealing with it, if they are used with the enthusiasm and public support which the situation requires ... I dragged out one figure after another into the daylight, I had to endure those silly debates with academics, and self-appointed experts, explaining that it was just a momentary scare ...

[*Blackout.*]

THE END